Forgiving Ot

Published by Ali Gator Productions
Copyright © 2018 Ali Gator Productions, Second Edition,
First Published 2016

National Library of Australia Cataloguing–in-Publication (CIP) data:
Isfand Samyono, Forgiving Others
ISBN: 978-1-921772-33-7
For primary school age, Juvenile fiction, Dewey Number: 823.92

Adapted from the original title Indahnya Memaafkan first published by Dar! Mizan.
Copyright© 2009 by Author Isfand Samyono, Illustrator Studio Air.Printed in Indonesia.

T: +61 (3) 9386 2771 F: +61 (3) 9478 8854
P.O. Box 2536, Regent West, Melbourne Victoria, 3072 Australia
E: info@ali-gator.com W: www.ali-gator.com

The aim of the Akhlaaq Building for Kids Series is to inspire young children to develop good Akhlaaq (manners) through fun stories involving young children like themselves.

The main characters are a young girl Saaliha and her younger brother Ali.

Along with their friends they experience various situations, all with a moral message for the young readers.

In Sha Allah (God Willing) if this series helps to inspire our young readers to be better people, following the best of example in manners and behavior, the Prophet Muhammad (peace be upon him), then we have truly achieved our goal.

BISMILLAHIR RAHMANIR RAHIM
IN THE NAME OF ALLAH, MOST GRACIOUS, MOST MERCIFUL

"Ali, let's go and play at Bilal's house," invited Faisal.

"No, I don't want to go anymore to Bilal's house," replied an unhappy Ali.

"Why don't you want to go to Bilal's house, he's your friend?"asked Faisal.

"You don't understand. Yesterday Bilal pushed me over in the playground and made me hurt myself," answered Ali.

"Yes, I do Ali, don't you remember? Last year when we were playing and Bilal hit me on the head with his racket and I hurt my head," explained Faisal.

9

"Then Bilal came to my house and apologized.
He said he was sorry and that it was an accident.

He told me that I was his friend
and that he would never try
to hurt me on purpose,"
said Faisal.

This made Ali think.
"Mmm... Maybe Bilal didn't mean to push me over. Maybe it was also an accident," said a very happy Ali.

"Well then let's go over to Bilal's house," said an even happier Faisal.

Faisal is a good example to Ali as he is a very forgiving person.

Faisal forgave his younger brother when he was playing with his toy boat and he accidentally lost it at the pond.

14

Faisal also forgave his friend Ahmed
when he forgot to come
and visit Faisal at his house.

So Faisal called Ahmed and went
to Ahmed's house instead.

Faisal knows that he also makes mistakes, and when he does he knows his friends will forgive him.

True friends don't hold grudges.

They have patience and understanding for each other, as no one is perfect.

19

Faisal loves his mother,
as she is a very forgiving lady.

She is the best example for Faisal,
as she is always kind to her family and friends.

Because Faisal is a forgiving person he has many friends.

Ali and his friends like it that Faisal forgives them if they make a mistake, because everyone makes mistakes.

ALHAMDULILLAH
PRAISE BE TO ALLAH